D0340333

Fic
BERNHEIM

SA FEMME

or THE OTHER WOMAN

EMMANUELE BERNHEIM

Translated from the French by Shaun Whiteside

VIKING

VIKING

Published by the Penguin Group
Penguin Books Ltd, 27 Wrights Lane, London W8 5TZ, England
Penguin Books USA Inc., 375 Hudson Street, New York, New York 10014, USA
Penguin Books Australia Ltd, Ringwood, Victoria, Australia
Penguin Books Canada Ltd, 10 Alcorn Avenue, Toronto, Ontario, Canada M4V 3B2
Penguin Books (NZ) Ltd, 182–190 Wairau Road, Auckland 10, New Zealand

Penguin Books Ltd, Registered Offices: Harmondsworth, Middlesex, England

First published in France by Editions Gallimard 1993
First published in Great Britain by Viking 1994
3 5 7 9 10 8 6 4 2

Set in 11/15.5pt Linotron Bodoni by
Rowland Phototypesetting Ltd, Bury St Edmunds, Suffolk
Printed in Great Britain by Clays Ltd, St Ives plc

A CIP catalogue record for this book is available from the British Library

ISBN 0-670-85811-0

Somebody had stolen her handbag.

She was having breakfast at the counter as she did every morning. She was eating her tartines, drinking her coffee, her handbag on the floor at her feet, pressed between her ankles. And it had disappeared. Somebody had stolen it and she hadn't felt a thing. None of the other customers had noticed anything, and neither had the café owner. No one had seen anything.

Claire got a copy of her keys from the concierge and climbed the stairs without waiting for the lift.

The first thing she did was to report the theft of her credit card; then she called a locksmith, who promised to come and change her lock at lunchtime.

When she had hung up she relaxed. It wasn't that serious. There hadn't been much money in her wallet and she hadn't had her cheque-book with her. As for her appointment book, it was there on the desk, next to the telephone.

She switched on the lamp in the waiting-room and tidied the pile of magazines. It was five to nine, and the first patient of the morning would be arriving soon.

The old man was taking a course of antibiotics, and he now had a fungal infection. His tongue was black. Claire was examining it when the doorbell rang again. She went to answer it. It was a young man. He was smiling. She asked him to wait and quickly went back into the surgery. On the way, she glanced automatically at her appointment book. She frowned – the next patient was a woman. So who was the man she had just let in? Probably an emergency. She went back to her patient and palpated his stomach. The infection had not yet reached his digestive tract. Then Claire stiffened. The stranger was whistling, whistling loudly. And cheerfully. He wasn't ill. No one who was ill would whistle like that in a waiting-room.

2

Perhaps it was the man who had stolen her bag. It had to be him. He had only found two hundred francs in Claire's wallet. It wasn't enough. He had seen her papers, he knew she was a doctor and he wanted the money from her consultations. He was waiting for her to be alone. While the old man was getting dressed, Claire half-opened a drawer in her desk. Her hand closed over the cold little body of a tear-gas spray. She slipped it into her pocket.

The stranger abruptly stopped whistling.

When Claire walked her patient to the door, the man had disappeared.

She leaned against the door, breathing deeply. It was then that she spotted her handbag on a cushion, clearly visible in the middle of the sofa. Her stolen handbag.

All that was missing was the money and the credit card.

Claire cancelled the locksmith, and prepared to welcome the next patient, an otitis case.

It was eight o'clock. As she did every evening after her last consultation, Claire lingered in her surgery. She considered the tiny surgery, the gleaming steel of the stirrups on the table, the instruments and phials neatly lined up in the glass-fronted case. She sat down in one of the two armchairs meant for the patients, and she looked around as someone consulting her for the first time would do. The framed posters, the lamps, the books, the carpet, she liked it all.

Claire closed her eyes. She was happy. The weather was growing colder. Soon cases of flu, angina and bronchitis would be proliferating.

Autumn and winter were her favourite seasons.

*

The flat had been divided into two. The consulting-room occupied the larger part, and Claire lived in the smaller part.

The communicating door was half-open. Claire sighed. Michel was there already.

She had left him two years before to live on her own, but they saw each other several times a week. And Michel had a duplicate set of keys.

She walked in silently. He was lying on the bed, not reading, not watching television, not even sleeping. He wasn't doing anything. He was waiting for her.

She gave a little cough. He saw her, stood up and came to kiss her. Then, as he always did, he stared at her.

'You look tired.'

And he ran her a bath.

Claire lived in a single room with bare white walls. A sliding door hid the corner where the kitchen was. The cupboards and the wardrobe were in the bathroom.

She slid into the hot water.

She heard the ice-cubes clinking in a glass. Michel was humming. Claire knew that he was always happy when she looked tired or worried or sad. He thought it brought her closer to him.

Even on the phone she heard his tones of satisfaction when he noticed her voice was faint.

She got out of her bath and dried herself vigorously. She would call the locksmith again tomorrow. She would tell him that she had had a think about it and that, although she had found her keys, she preferred to have the lock changed, just to be on the safe side.

She would have new keys. And this time she wouldn't give a set to Michel.

The locksmith had worked cleanly, without scratching the paint on the door. He had left three sets of keys. Claire put one of them on her key-ring, left the second with the concierge and placed the third in a drawer in her desk.

She spent the evening alone. Her fridge was full. Claire pulled a face. She still had some pork chops.

She had opened her surgery two years before and, after a difficult first year, she had decided to get to know the local shopkeepers. Although she hadn't much money, she went shopping every day. Now the shopkeepers and their customers knew her; in the shops, and sometimes even in the street, they told her about their complaints and she listened to them attentively. And they came to consult her. So she had managed to build up a thriving practice.

But the groceries accumulated. She had dinner at home every evening and often invited friends around so as not to waste anything.

She cooked a pork chop.

She would sleep badly, as she did every evening, because, living in a single room, the smells of cooking permeated even her sheets.

Claire woke with a start. The windows were rattling, the floor was vibrating. Her alarm clock was ringing and she could hardly hear it, the noise outside was so loud. She got up and opened the shutters. Her neighbours, in pyjamas or night-dresses, were at their windows.

Some years earlier, a fire had destroyed a nearby building. Now they were starting to rebuild it.

The noise wouldn't disturb her too much; her surgery overlooked the courtyard and she would get some earplugs.

Claire went out to do her shopping, as she did every day at midday. Three men were talking in front of the big hoarding that hid the building site. Two of them went away but the third stayed where he was. Claire thought she recognized him as the man who had returned her bag. He disappeared into the building site.

She stopped in front of a little door cut into the hoarding. 'No trespassing.' 'Hard-hat zone.' In the street, red and white cones prohibited parking. Claire hesitated. Then she opened the little door and closed it behind her again.

The interior of the burned-out building was being piled into skips. Broken windows, charred shutters, eviscerated mattresses and rusty household implements lay in the middle of the rubble. The hubbub was deafening. Each crash made her wince. The dust made the air unbreathable. Suddenly a man appeared in an opening in the façade. He shouted something to Claire. She couldn't hear a thing. Then he made big, vehement gestures and she understood that he was asking her to leave. She turned towards the hoarding but she couldn't find the door. Abruptly silence fell. Claire put her hands to her ears – she thought she must have gone deaf. But then she heard some rubble moving and calmed down.

A man emerged from the building. He was wearing a yellow helmet and a surgeon's mask. Crossing the courtyard, he took off his helmet and lowered his mask. He smiled. It was him. His fore-head and eyebrows were grey with dust. He ruffled his hair, which had been flattened by the helmet. Claire smiled too. She apologized for disturbing him – she just wanted to thank him for the handbag.

He had found it there, on the ground, just behind the hoarding.

He put his hand on the door handle. Claire thanked him again. He opened the door. She was about to go when he tapped her on the back. She turned round.

'There was dust on your jacket.'

She felt herself blushing. She said thank you again, and left the site.

For a moment she didn't know where she was; then she recognized the street. She thought she was late and ran towards her building. In the lift, she looked at her watch. It was just past midday. She had only been on the other side of the hoarding for a few minutes.

She pressed the button to go down to the ground floor again and went to do her shopping.

In the chemist's they had already sold out of earplugs.

The patients followed one after another until the evening. After the last consultation, Claire slumped into one of the armchairs. She took off her shoes, noticed the dust on them and remembered the dusty brow of the man on the building site. She ran her fingers along the leather, and then slowly rubbed her thumb against her index finger. It was soft.

The doorbell made her jump. She hadn't told Michel about changing the locks – she would say she had only one set of keys. She opened the door to him. He barely looked at her. She wanted to speak to him but gave up the idea. He wouldn't listen to her. He knew already that she was going to lie.

They ate the last of the pork chops, and he left early.

She was coming out of the butcher's when she saw him. He was calling to her from the opposite pavement: 'Doctor!' He ran across the street, took Claire by the arm and led her towards a café. She went with him, her bag of groceries dangling between them.

His name was Thomas Kovacs and he was a contractor. She asked him about the building under reconstruction. He put three lumps of sugar in his coffee. He never stopped moving. He put his elbows on the table and then threw himself against the back of his chair and stretched his arms out behind him. Twice he had to turn and apologize for bumping into somebody. Claire watched him, but without hearing what he said. He was probably forty-two or forty-three. With his spoon, he scraped at the sediment of sugar at the bottom of his cup. Suddenly he grabbed Claire's left wrist to see the time on her watch. He would have to go. He beckoned the waiter, paid and stood up. He leaned towards her. He seemed to freeze. He looked at her, his eyes shining. Then he said, 'See you tomorrow', and he disappeared.

Claire went home. She felt as though she was walking in slow motion.

In her right hand she was clutching a sugar cube. She didn't throw it away.

It was Saturday. The building work stopped at the weekend. Claire wouldn't be seeing Thomas Kovacs today.

She opened the top drawer of her desk and thrust her hand inside. She took out four sugar cubes, lined them up and looked at them.

Each sugar cube corresponded to a meeting with him, in the café, at lunchtime.

She worked until five and Michel came to get her. They had been invited to the country.

It was a sociable evening. Claire was in a good mood and Michel didn't take his eyes off her. When she met his gaze, she turned away immediately and went on laughing with the others. He went to bed first. She watched him slowly climbing the stairs.

He had put out the light. Claire crossed the room on tiptoe and slid between the sheets. She curled up at the edge of the bed so as not to hear Michel breathing, not to brush against his big body. He was asleep. He was breathing with difficulty, through his mouth, as if his nose was blocked, sniffing gently. Then she noticed little movements shaking the mattress. Michel wasn't asleep. He didn't have a cold. He was crying. Claire didn't move towards him. She didn't move.

He went back to Paris after breakfast.

Claire went for a walk in the forest on her own. She snapped dead branches under her feet, and she splashed about in the mud. She realized that she was singing at the top of her voice.

At lunch, she ate a lot.

The first thing she did when she got home was to unplug the big halogen lamp, a present from Michel. She put it in the wardrobe. She didn't like its white light.

She listened to the messages on her answering machine. Michel hadn't called.

The fridge was almost empty. Since she had been seeing Thomas Kovacs at lunchtime she no longer had the time to do her shopping. Claire looked around her. For the first time, she liked her room.

She felt at home.

On Monday he didn't turn up for their meeting.

After waiting for him, Claire lingered by the hoarding beside the building site. There wasn't a sound; it was lunchtime. She didn't dare push open the little door.

She went back up to her flat, got her black bag and went out again. Her hands were cold. She would have to warm them up before examining a patient. The two coffees that she had drunk while waiting for Thomas Kovacs were burning her stomach. She went into a baker's shop and saw herself in the mirror. She was thirty, but she tried to look older. Young doctors don't inspire confidence. She was wearing a grey suit and hardly any make-up.

She was grey. And that was how Thomas saw her.

She left the baker's without buying anything.

As soon as she got to her consulting-room, Claire relaxed. The room was well heated and the shutters and the window, which was closed, muffled the noises of the street. She approached the couch and sounded the patient's chest. 'Deep breath. Open wide.' Claire spoke in a hushed voice, the room was so quiet. From the sheets there rose a smell of fresh laundry.

She threw the tongue depressor into the wastepaper basket and put her instruments in order. It was flu. She sat down to write out the prescription. She wrote slowly, taking her time. She was absorbing the calm and warmth of the room.

Claire never felt as good as she did in a sickroom.

The next day, Claire came upon the sugar cubes lined up in the drawer. Then she remembered Thomas's broad smile, his neck when he threw back his head to drink the last drops of his sweet coffee. She felt again the warmth of his hand when he took her wrist to see the time. And at their last meeting, on Friday, his chestnut hair seemed grey, it was so dusty.

She took the sugar cubes and threw them in her waste-paper basket. What was the point of keeping them? She wouldn't be seeing Thomas Kovacs again.

She didn't leave the building at lunchtime.

*

Night fell. Claire was taking a young man's blood pressure when the phone rang. She picked it up and immediately recognized Thomas's voice. He wanted to see her, as soon as he could. That evening. She had another two patients. He would wait for her in a bar nearby.

Claire opened her wardrobe. She had few clothes. They were almost all grey, because grey goes with everything. She closed the door immediately. From the dirty laundry basket she took the jeans that she had worn in the country. There was some dried mud at the bottom of the legs. Claire scratched and rubbed, but brown traces remained. Nevertheless, she put on the jeans, a navy blue pullover and tennis shoes. Then she put on her make-up. She looked at herself in the mirror. She wasn't grey now.

She went quickly down the stairs. She was about to push open the door of the building when she froze, ran back to her flat and dashed into the surgery. She rummaged about in the waste-paper basket, took out the four sugar cubes and put them back in the desk drawer. A little later that evening, the concierge would come to do the cleaning. She would empty the bins. And Claire would never have seen her sugar cubes again.

She slammed the door and tore down the stairs.

When he saw her, Thomas didn't smile. He didn't get up. He didn't move. Claire sat down opposite him. On the table, there was no glass or cup, not even a paper mat for under the saucer. Thomas hadn't drunk anything.

The barman appeared immediately. She ordered a Bloody Mary, Thomas didn't want anything. He stayed silent. She didn't dare speak first, because she suddenly realized she couldn't remember how they addressed each other. The barman brought her cocktail straight away. She stared at her glass, and spent a long time mixing its contents with a little yellow plastic golf club. She tried to think of a sentence in which she wouldn't have to use '*tu*' or '*vous*'.

Abruptly, Thomas grabbed her wrist, her right wrist, to stop the golf club moving. He leaned towards her. He had something very important to tell her.

He gripped her wrist hard.

He hadn't kept the appointment, but it was not

because he didn't want to see her. On the contrary, he wanted to see her constantly, every day. But he couldn't, he mustn't.

'Why?'

'Because I have a wife and two children. I will never leave them. And I can't make you suffer.'

Claire said nothing. He let go of her wrist. She didn't move her arm. It stayed on the table, motionless. Her skin, warmed by Thomas's hand, was already cooling down.

Even if she could expect nothing from him, she wanted to go on seeing him.

Finally he smiled. The white of his eyes was very white.

He paid the barman and got up. He had to go home.

They left the bar. He kissed Claire on the lips, very quickly. She watched him going away. He was almost running. She would have liked to see his car but he disappeared around a corner.

Claire went to meet some friends in a restaurant.

She whistled as she walked.

She had taken the little yellow golf club.

The next day, leaving the café, they stopped and faced each other for a moment. Fog was escaping Thomas's half-open lips, and his breath smelled of coffee. The inside of his mouth would be hot, and it was bound to taste of sweet coffee. They didn't kiss. Two workers from the building site, standing at the bar, were watching them through the glass. And on the opposite pavement, an old woman sitting under a bus shelter smiled at Claire. It was one of her patients.

They parted.

They decided not to meet at the café any more, but at Claire's flat, in the evening, after surgery.

*

Thomas would come at eight. Claire was staring at the clock in her consulting-room. It was twenty to eight, her last patient was ten minutes late.

At last she came. She was very pale and seemed to be in pain. She sat down carefully in one of the two armchairs and rested her left arm on the armrest with a grimace.

Claire asked her what was wrong. She was thirty, and a cashier at the nearby supermarket. Through constantly repeating the same movement with her left arm, passing each article over the bar-code reader, she was getting terrible pains running from her neck to her hand. And every day the pain got worse. She couldn't take her clothes off on her own any more. Claire helped her gently and examined her.

Cervicobrachial neuralgia. She prescribed an anti-inflammatory and an analgesic. And an X-ray of the spinal column. She gave her ten days' sick leave.

The young woman asked if she might stay in the waiting-room because her husband was coming to collect her in the car. They lived a long way away.

25

Claire settled her on the sofa and supported her back with cushions.

The bell rang again. It was Thomas.

She ushered him into her room and closed the door behind him. She put some magazines beside her patient and went back to Thomas.

They whispered. They looked at each other, they smiled at each other. But they didn't kiss. Claire listened to the sounds coming from the waiting-room. She heard nothing, not even the faint rustle of the pages of a magazine. Nothing. The young woman wasn't reading. She must be on the sofa, in the position where Claire had left her, upright and motionless, not daring to move for fear of starting the pain off again.

Her husband didn't come to get her until half-past eight.

Thomas left a few minutes later.

Claire was on her own.

From now on, she wouldn't see any more patients after seven.

26

Whether he was lying on top of her or she on him, their mouths never parted.

If the right arm of one escaped their mingled bodies, the left hand of the other immediately brought it back.

They were almost the same height. Thus, from their toes to their foreheads, Thomas was glued to Claire, and Claire was glued to Thomas.

He got dressed. She stayed in bed.

He leaned over her and kissed her again.

Then he disappeared.

Claire heard a car start. She dashed to the window but saw nothing.

The bumpers, the wings and the bottom of the doors of Thomas's car would be covered with the mud of the building sites. And it must have four doors because of the children.

Suddenly the room seemed very quiet. There was nothing to tidy up. No glass to rinse because Thomas hadn't drunk anything, no wet towel to dry because he hadn't washed. No trace of Thomas. Only the bedspread was a bit crumpled. Then Claire saw, beside the bed, a torn gold paper wrapper. She picked it up and smiled. In the bathroom she put her foot on the pedal of the bin. The lid rose. At the bottom of the almost empty bin lay something small, round and gleaming. Claire knelt down and picked it up, the condom that Thomas had used.

She put it back in its torn wrapper. And she tidied it away in her desk drawer, with the sugar cubes and the golf club.

She wouldn't have dinner at home. She hadn't replaced Michel's halogen lamp. The room was dark.

She went to dine alone in a brightly lit brasserie.

The waiters bustled around her and she joked with them.

The chips were so good that she ordered a second portion.

Claire woke up aching all over.

Every time she moved, her muscles felt sensitive; she kept getting up all the time.

All day she was uncomfortably aware of her aching bones.

She listened to the noise of the workmen. Sometimes, through the hubbub, a single voice could be heard. Maybe it was Thomas's.

At midday, she bought some champagne, some pastis and some fruit juice. She already had some whisky and beer, brought by Michel.

Thomas could choose what he wanted.

*

Before he arrived, she took one of the lamps from her surgery and plugged it in in her room. She replaced it with Michel's.

The moment he came in, Thomas embraced Claire.

They didn't drink anything.

He left. Claire put her face to the pillow where his head had lain, and sniffed. She couldn't find Thomas's smell there. She couldn't smell anything.

She got up, switched on the television and turned up the sound.

Then she noticed that she was mechanically rubbing her thighs against each other, but to no purpose. Because of the condom, there was none of Thomas's sperm running between her legs.

Her aches had disappeared.

She stayed motionless for a moment in the middle of the room.

Suddenly she came to herself. She grabbed her address book. She was going to ring up all her friends, even the ones she hadn't seen for ages.

She would go out every evening so she wouldn't be alone after Thomas had gone.

31

She flicked through her notebook. At the letter K she stopped, looking at the names shown there. With careful handwriting, she wrote KOVACS Thomas. She drew back slightly, Six letters, twice. The O and the A of the first name echoed those of the surname. Thomas Kovacs. That sounded good.

She picked up the phone book. She found about forty Kovacses but no Thomas.

He probably lived in the suburbs. In a house with a garden. He would have built it himself or perhaps just done it up. He had built a garage for his car and the other one, the two-door, which belonged to his wife. Here too they would keep their four bicycles, lined up along the wall, from the biggest to the smallest.

Claire closed the phone book again, consulted her address book and picked up the phone. She would be careful not to accept any dinner invitations before nine o'clock.

On Saturday, after surgery, Claire decided to go and buy herself some perfume.

In a big department store she went from display to display, sometimes spotting the scent of one of her patients. When she was starting to get a migraine she chose an eau de toilette that she thought was delicate enough.

She also bought a black jumper and a black skirt, a short one. She was barely out of the shop before she regretted her purchase. Thomas paid no attention to Claire's clothes. He didn't have time. The moment he arrived, he pressed her to him. They crossed the waiting-room kissing, locked in such a close embrace that they trod on each other's

33

toes, practically falling over. It made them laugh, teeth against teeth. Finally they would try to undress without interrupting their kisses. She didn't get dressed again until Thomas had gone.

So when and how would he notice what she was wearing?

Michel insisted on helping her choose her clothes. She had never listened to his advice. He always advised her to buy whatever suited her least. He probably wanted nobody else but him to fancy her.

When she'd got back, she put on some perfume and her new clothes. The phone rang. The minute she heard Michel's voice, Claire involuntarily pulled her black skirt down to cover her thighs. He apologized for his silence. He had been doing a lot of thinking and he absolutely had to see her and speak to her. She agreed to have lunch with him the following day.

When he had hung up, she started to undo her skirt. Suddenly she changed her mind, and pulled the zip back up.

She was free to wear whatever she wanted.

*

34

She had dinner at the home of Marie, her best friend.

Marie had given birth two months earlier, but she was now as slim as she had been before her pregnancy. Claire went into the baby's room. Bernard, the father, was leaning over the cradle. He didn't raise his head when Claire came in. He was humming or murmuring something. She watched him. He still wasn't aware of her presence.

How old were Thomas's children? They were probably little, and at that very moment Thomas was telling them a story or singing them a lullaby, a Hungarian lullaby. And he heard nothing but their light breathing, he saw nothing but their closing eyes.

Claire picked up a musical doll and pulled on the string. Hearing the music, Bernard stood up.

'He's asleep.'

They left the room.

She rejoined Marie in the kitchen. There were baby-bottles everywhere.

Claire wouldn't talk to her about Thomas.

Michel noticed immediately that the halogen lamp wasn't there. Claire took him into her consulting-room; he saw it there and seemed reassured. But once they were back in the room, he sat down on the bed and looked around, searching for the slightest alteration. She followed his eyes. He wouldn't find anything because nothing had changed. Not even Claire. She wasn't wearing make-up or perfume. She had on clothes that he knew and her face was dull, she could feel it, as it was every time she saw Michel.

He cleared his throat; he was going to speak to her. But first he got up to get something to drink. Claire smiled faintly. She went into the bathroom, leaving the door half-open, and listened.

He opens the sliding door; then the fridge door. Behind the yoghurts and the butter-dish he finds a beer. Psht. He has just pulled the ring-pull. He discovers the fruit juices. That surprises him, because Claire never drinks them. Now he sees the bottle of champagne. But Claire doesn't like it – someone must have brought it for her. The fridge door closes again. He takes a glass from above the sink. On the shelf next to it he notices the pastis. Silence.

He slowly closes the sliding door.

He has understood.

Claire emerged from the bathroom.

Michel didn't ask her any questions. And he didn't say what he had to say to her.

They had lunch at the restaurant. Michel relaxed. She watched him. He even seemed relieved, now he knew that it was over between them.

Claire walked out with her last patient of the day. She pressed the automatic light switch and called the lift. The patient went in and the metal door closed behind him. A noise made Claire jump. She turned round. Thomas was sitting on the stairs, his eyes shining. He jumped up and embraced her. He pressed her to him and spoke to her gently. He had missed her for those two days, and was in such a hurry to see her again that he had waited for her there, in the dark, hoping that she would stop work earlier than usual. Then he broke away from her and called the lift again. Today he wanted to go to the café. Claire went back quickly for her handbag and her coat.

SA FEMME

She was sorry she couldn't wear her new clothes because Thomas would have time to look at her in the café.

They sat down opposite one another. She ordered a whisky. Thomas wasn't thirsty. He didn't say anything. He hardly looked at her. And yet just now, he had seemed so happy to be with her again. He started rubbing at a patch of paint on his left hand. When it was gone he raised his eyes to Claire and, finally, smiled at her. He moved closer to the table until their knees met. He asked her about her work. She liked talking about it, and talked about it for a long time. He listened to her without taking his eyes off her.

She drank her whisky and abruptly, almost involuntarily, she asked him what his wife did for a living. She saw him hesitate.

'She's an architect.'

Then he looked at the watch on Claire's wrist. He would have to be getting back.

They parted in front of her building. He kissed her on the lips, very quickly.

*

She fell on to the bed. Why would he want to go to the café when he'd been so much looking forward to seeing her? And she should never have asked him that question about his wife. He didn't want to talk about his family, it was obvious. He didn't want to cause Claire any pain.

But what if he decided not to come back, never to see her again?

She plunged her face between her hands. Impossible. In the café, Thomas's knees had been pressing so hard against hers that the fine web of her stockings was surely printed on his skin.

She would see him again, she was sure of it.

She took a deep breath. Although she had washed her hands countless times in the course of the day, the scent of the eau de toilette on her wrists remained.

Claire stood up again. She had understood. Thomas had pulled away from her because of her perfume. He was afraid of the scent permeating his clothes and his skin. His wife would surely have smelled it. That was why he had taken Claire to the café.

*

Claire wasn't mistaken.

She stopped wearing perfume. And Thomas stopped taking her to the café.

Thomas's wife had probably designed the house, and he had built it.

On the ground floor, the sitting-room, vast and very light, a kitchen with an enormous table, and no dining-room. No, the sitting-room and the kitchen weren't separate. They formed a single big room. That way, when they had company, Thomas's wife would be able to prepare the meal while taking part in the conversation.

She was sure to be a very good cook, and their friends liked going to their house for dinner. The Kovacs's house.

Whatever time he arrived, Thomas stayed at Claire's for an hour and a quarter. Never more, seldom less.

One day, she unplugged her video recorder and her electric coffee-maker and hid her alarm clock in the drawer of the bedside table. That way Thomas wouldn't have any way of knowing the time and he would stay for longer.

When he rang the doorbell, before going to let him in, Claire would look at the time on her watch and put it in her handbag. It was twenty-five to eight.

They were lying side by side.

Claire listened to Thomas's breathing. For the first time, forgetting what time it was, perhaps he would fall asleep next to her. She didn't move. His skin was growing moist in the places where their bodies touched. She closed her eyes. They would spend the night together and, tomorrow, they would have breakfast together. Thomas probably ate a lot in the morning. She had eggs, cheese and two slices of ham. That would do. She wouldn't open the window, and all day the flat would smell of toast.

Thomas pressed himself against her and kissed her gently. Then he drew away from her and got up.

When she closed the front door behind him, it was ten to nine.

Thomas had stayed with her for an hour and a quarter, an hour and a quarter to the minute.

Claire would stop unplugging her appliances.

From now on the alarm clock would stay on her bedside table, and the watch on her wrist.

Claire switched on her bedside light. It was half-past six in the morning.

At this moment, Thomas is probably having his breakfast. He's probably made the coffee. His wife comes and joins him. She is wearing her husband's dressing-gown, which is too big for her. Her long hair is all in tangles. Thomas smiles at her – he thinks she's beautiful. One of the children comes into the kitchen. His mother tells him off for being barefoot. He climbs on to his father's lap. Thomas takes the child's two feet in one of his hands and warms them up. He begins to put his three sugar cubes in his coffee, or maybe four because the breakfast cups are bigger. The child stops him, wanting to put them in himself. He drops them from too high up and coffee splashes on the table.

Thomas is about to go. The car will disappear into the distance. On the back seat, his yellow helmet for the building site.

He kisses his wife. Their mouths taste of coffee.

'See you this evening.'

Claire goes back to sleep.

She opened her eyes when the builders started, and got up.

During the week, she never used her alarm clock. She didn't need it. The noise of the building site woke her up. And she almost imagined she could hear Thomas there.

Claire was palpating a patient's abdomen. He was about Thomas's age and wore a wedding ring. Thomas didn't wear one. He was probably afraid of losing it on a building site. The man complained of stomach pains. He had never had his appendix out. Neither had Thomas. Claire would have seen his scar.

Thomas never fell ill, she was sure. He didn't cough, he didn't blow his nose, he didn't even sniff. No liver problems, not a hint of yellow to tinge the white of his eyes. On the building sites he worked hard, he doubtless lifted heavy things but he didn't have back pains, or sciatica, or the slightest lumbago. And he never had migraines. Nothing.

The patient got dressed.

Claire sat down at her desk.

She would have liked to treat Thomas. She would know his blood count, his cholesterol level and, from the atlas to the sacrum, she would see each one of his vertebrae. As with this patient, she would refer him for an X-ray of his digestive tract. Then she would discover Thomas's oesophagus, his stomach, each fold of his small intestine and the bulges in his large intestine, his whole digestive system made almost phosphorescent by the barium meal.

But he was never ill.

Claire sighed. All she knew was the smooth skin of Thomas's belly.

She had never even seen him eating, or drinking, apart from sweet coffee. She didn't know anything about his likes and dislikes. If he took that much sugar in his coffee, he would certainly have a taste for puddings. But she couldn't imagine him eating cakes. No, he's bound to prefer meat, stew, game. And when he's finished he wipes his plate with a piece of bread.

Claire easily imagines him sitting on a breeze-block, near a stove on the building site. He's eating a chicken drumstick with his fingers. The gristle crunches between his teeth. He's hungry, he eats quickly, he digests everything.

Does his wife sometimes make him up a lunch-box? In the morning she fills it up with yesterday's leftovers and seals it. She smiles. It reminds her of the early days of their marriage, when Thomas was still a foreman. The children look on enviously – they'd like a lunch-box to take to school. They'd make a wood fire to heat it up, and they wouldn't have to go to the dining hall.

Claire gave a start. Her patient, ready to leave, was holding a cheque out to her. She took it and quickly filled in the social security form.

'Now, breathe normally . . . Perfect.'

Claire put down her stethoscope.

The siren of an ambulance rang out suddenly, getting closer and closer.

There must have been an accident. Maybe on the building site next door. Accidents happen frequently on building sites. Drills slip, ceilings crumble, girders collapse. Maybe a girder has fallen on Thomas. The labourers can't lift it off him. He's losing lots of blood. One more go and the girder lifts a bit, just enough to free him. The ambulance arrives, its wheels skid in the mud of the building site. They put Thomas on a stretcher. Carefully. Gently.

The patient held out her soft, tepid arm. Claire took her blood pressure. The skin of Thomas's forearm is so smooth, his veins are so prominent, it'll be easy for the ambulance men to put in the needle for the drip.

She pulled open the Velcro on the tourniquet. The young woman's blood pressure was normal.

Claire will cancel all her appointments to be near Thomas in hospital: she will check his drip, redo his bandages, examine his X-rays and give him his injections herself.

But she won't even know what hospital he has been taken to. And when Thomas opens his eyes his wife is the one he will see. She will hold him in her arms and he will breathe her perfume.

Because she wears perfume.

The patient glanced at her prescription and paid up with bad grace. Claire had only prescribed magnesium.

Claire found a message from Thomas on her private answering machine.

He was sorry, something had turned up, he wouldn't be able to come this evening.

Claire smiled. It was her first message from Thomas.

He never phoned her.

She turned up the sound on her answering machine and listened to it again. Thomas's voice was faint. He was almost whispering.

She didn't wind the tape back; she didn't want Thomas's message to be erased by a new one.

*

At lunchtime she bought some blank tapes. She replaced the one in the answering machine with one of the new ones and put the used one in the drawer of her desk.

From now on, she would keep every recording of Thomas's voice.

Thomas was pressed against her. She had closed her eyes, and smelled, in his hair, the smell of building-site dust.

Then Thomas's head grew heavier on her shoulder. He had gone to sleep. It was the first time he had gone to sleep beside her.

Thomas's breath was so warm and so thick against her neck that she felt sure a little circle of condensation was forming there.

Thomas's head grew heavier and heavier on her shoulder. She could almost feel each hair embedding itself in the skin of her cheek and her chin.

The arm resting on Claire's stomach changed position and stopped moving, the inside of the wrist against her navel. Thomas's pulse reverberated in her stomach. When Claire held her breath she felt the pulsing of Thomas's blood throughout her whole body.

The arm slipped slightly and then she couldn't feel anything any more.

She opened her eyes. Thomas's skin was smooth. No beauty spots, very little hair. His leg still bore the trace of the elastic of his sock, his feet were small and broad, and his little toe was shaped like a piece of a tangerine.

She smiled. Thomas woke up.

He jumped up and got dressed.

He pressed Claire to him but didn't kiss her. Then he went away.

She was left alone. He hadn't kissed her but he had held her in his arms more tightly than usual, and for longer. Claire was happy. The beginnings of Thomas's beard had left a red mark on her shoulder.

When he shaved, in the morning, long swathes of soft skin appeared in the white foam. Afterwards he probably had a shower – showers are quicker than baths. He had never washed at Claire's, although she had bought some unscented soap.

And she had never heard him flushing the toilet.

He probably washed before he went to bed. He soaped himself for a long time. He erased the smell of Claire's body. And then he slid into his bed, next to his wife.

Claire shivered. She got dressed.

The next morning, the red mark on her shoulder had disappeared.

The Christmas holidays were approaching.

Thomas would surely be going skiing with his wife and his children. He would cover his lips with total sunblock and his mouth would look almost white against his tanned face.

When he came back, the area around his eyes would be pale, because of his sunglasses. And the top of his forehead too, if he wore a ski hat – no, she couldn't imagine Thomas in a ski hat.

But when would he leave? And when would he come back?

She didn't know. He hadn't said anything about it yet and she never asked him any questions.

The escalator leading to the toy department was full. Claire clutched the handrail.

She still had to buy one Christmas present, for her nephew. What was he interested in? She didn't know anything about him, she never saw him. Nicolas was nine, and he hated her. When he was tiny, he screamed every time she went near him; now he sloped off and locked himself in his room the minute she arrived. So Claire went to see her sister very rarely, always late in the evening, when she was sure the child was asleep.

The steps of the escalator levelled out beneath her feet.

She let go of the black rubber rail and her hand was moist.

She couldn't even remember what Nicolas looked like.

A little boy bumped into her and apologized. He was smiling broadly, his hair tousled. He looked like Thomas. Maybe it was his son. He went back to a long-haired woman holding a little girl by the hand.

She was Thomas's wife, and they were his children, Claire was certain of it.

She followed them into the crowd.

She could only see the young woman from behind. She was wearing a fur jacket. Claire moved closer, and her hand reached out to touch it. The fur was soft, almost hot.

Suddenly the little boy pointed his finger at a man coming towards them, and ran to throw himself into his arms.

The four of them walked away, their arms around each other.

Claire looked about her. There were little boys everywhere, and they all looked like Thomas.

She bought a computer game for Nicolas and quickly left the shop.

Claire woke with a start. Her doorbell had rung.

Half-past eight, her first patient.

Why hadn't she woken up?

She quickly slipped on the previous day's clothes, and hurried to open the door. She brought the patient into her surgery, apologized and ran into the bathroom to brush her teeth. Then she froze. She could hardly hear anything. Nothing at all. She dashed to the window and opened it. The street was silent. Then Claire understood why she hadn't woken up: there was no building work this morning.

And what if Thomas had left without telling her?

Her patient gave a start when she touched him – her hands were freezing.

*

Between two patients she went into the street. The pavement had been swept in front of the hoarding. Claire went towards the little door. The handle had disappeared. The site was closed.

As soon as she could she went to listen to the answering machine on her private line. There were no messages from Thomas.

She couldn't remember whether, the previous day, he had said, 'See you tomorrow.' She could only remember that they had been so closely mingled that she suddenly hadn't known whether she was stroking her own skin or Thomas's.

After her last patient left, Claire slumped on to the sofa in her waiting-room.

She didn't move. Thomas wouldn't be coming. He had left this morning, in his big four-door saloon. In the back, the children were whingeing. Their seat-belts were too tight. They've probably arrived by now. Thomas's wife is opening their bags. She hasn't forgotten a thing. She's even thought about bringing some spaghetti for dinner and coffee for breakfast. Thomas kisses her on the neck. Tomorrow they'll go shopping, all four of them.

Claire got up slowly and returned to her surgery.

She opened the first drawer in her desk. The sugar cubes, the golf club and the cassette from her answering machine were still there. They lay on a carpet of little gold squares. The wrappers of the condoms, all empty, except the first one.

Claire had never thrown any of them away.

She started counting them.

Thirty-five, thirty-six, thirty-seven, thirty-eight. She felt better.

Fifty-nine, sixty, sixty-one. The doorbell interrupted her. Maybe it was Thomas. She put the gold wrappers, higgledy-piggledy, back in the drawer and closed it.

Thomas was holding a bouquet of roses.

He took Claire in his arms.

She heard the paper wrapping of the flowers rustling against her back.

She freed herself and he gave her the bouquet.

She put some water in a vase and arranged the roses one by one. A dozen. It was the first time that Thomas had brought her flowers. Why today? Probably because he was leaving tomorrow.

He approached her, embraced her again, but she pulled away from him.

He was leaving tomorrow, wasn't he? He stared at her.

Until the beginning of January then? He grew very pale, turned round and walked towards the door.

Claire held him back.

She put her hands on his neck, where the skin is so smooth, and she kissed him. He closed his eyes. Suddenly his breathing changed. Each time Claire breathed out, he breathed in. They kissed for a long time. She could feel Thomas's throat pulsing beneath the palms of her hands.

He was breathing Claire's breath. And he was drinking her saliva.

There were so many people on the train that Claire had to travel with her presents on her knees.

Her neighbour held a bag of groceries pressed against her. A long vacuum-packed salmon was sticking out of the bag.

In previous years Michel had gone with her, in the car. Her parents had been disappointed to learn that she was coming to celebrate Christmas without him. Her whole family liked Michel. It was always Michel that Nicolas thanked for the presents which Claire had given him. She tried to relax. Nicolas was older now – maybe he would stop running away from her.

And she hadn't seen her parents for a long time;

her mother would be pleased to see her.

Next to her, her neighbour was falling asleep.

For the duration of the journey, the cardboard wrapper of the salmon rubbed against Claire's arm.

She lifted her head. The electric lights around the Christmas tree twinkled through the curtains. Claire stayed motionless on the footpath.

Only when she grew very cold did she decide to go inside.

She rang the bell and immediately heard Nicolas running away. When she got in, he had disappeared.

Her father, her mother, her sister Sylvie and Jean-Paul, her brother-in-law: she kissed them all.

Her mother didn't even notice that Claire's cheeks were freezing.

She laid her parcels under the Christmas tree. Coloured wrapping paper was scattered over the floor. She supposed that Nicolas had been allowed to open his presents before she arrived, probably for fear that she would spoil the child's pleasure by being there.

Sylvie drew her into the kitchen and asked her in a low voice for some Valium. But Claire hadn't brought her prescription pad. Her sister seemed annoyed. In silence, she cut open the plastic wrapper of a packet of smoked salmon. Then they took the slices, separated by sheets of cellophane, and arranged them on a plate. Claire left the room. She noticed Sylvie's handbag on the drawing-room sofa, and went over and opened it. Her father and Jean-Paul, busy fixing one of Nicolas's toys, didn't see her. She quickly found what she was looking for, a little green box of Valium, almost empty. She swallowed half a tablet and put everything back in its place.

Nicolas seemed to like the computer game. He thanked Claire and allowed her to kiss him on his hair.

Dinner was ready. Nicolas sat next to his father and played with Claire's present.

She didn't eat any salmon.

Tomorrow, as they had done every year since Nicolas was born, they would all be setting off for the Pyrenees. She couldn't quite listen to their conversation. They were making plans for New Year, and talking about friends she didn't know. Her mother's voice was the same as her sister's.

Then her eyes began to blink in time with the fairy lights, and all she could hear was the beep-beep of the video game. She shouldn't have taken the Valium, she wasn't used to tranquillizers. She tried to control the flickering of her eyelids. Her eyes fixed on a gleaming, orange surface. The salmon. The beeps grew further and further away. And she fell asleep.

The compartment was almost empty. She took a seat next to the window and stretched out her legs on the seat opposite. She felt good.

She had woken up lying on the sofa when they were on their dessert, a Christmas log. Her parents didn't seem worried about her. Doctors never really get ill. After they'd had coffee and exchanged their presents, she had kissed everyone. And she had gone downstairs on foot, without even waiting for the lift.

Then she had skipped all the way to the station.

When she got home she would put on a record. She wanted to hear some music.

Claire realized she was hungry.

Every day, she examined Thomas's roses. They had opened, but they weren't fading yet.

One morning, their heads began to droop. Claire wondered whether to cut off the ends of the stems.

Finally she went to get some scissors from the consulting room. They were Thomas's flowers. She couldn't let them wither like that. She carefully trimmed each of the twelve stems at an angle.

That evening, all the roses had perked up. Claire sighed. She would have to wait a few days before she could put them in her desk drawer.

*

She rushed to get her Polaroid camera from the wardrobe. Why hadn't she thought of it before?

She took a picture of the bouquet.

The colours were pale, but it was easy to make out the roses.

She put the photograph in the drawer. She was about to close it again, but changed her mind. She pulled it all the way out, removing it entirely, and put it on the desk. She moved the lamp further away, for the little squares of gold paper reflected too much light. And then she took a picture of the contents of the drawer.

When the photograph was ready, she slipped it into her wallet.

Claire went to the supermarket.

From a distance she saw her patient, the cashier. The young woman was wearing a surgical collar – had she been to see another doctor? In a minute, Claire would pass her cash desk and hear what had happened.

First she headed for the household goods department. Then she strolled around the aisles. She noticed a woman piling several boxes of sugar cubes into a trolley.

At Claire's flat, a box of sugar lasted almost six months.

She thought about Thomas's sweet coffee. If she

lived with him she would buy as much sugar as that woman did.

Suddenly she wanted to leave the shop.

All around her, people were pushing full trolleys. But Claire hadn't even taken a trolley. A metal basket was enough for all that she wanted to buy. She lived alone.

She would speak to her patient another time. She joined the shortest of the queues, the one reserved for customers with less than ten items.

She studied her diary. Every moment spent with Thomas was noted down in it. A big T and a double vertical arrow indicating the time of his arrival and the time of his departure.

Claire took a sheet of paper and a pencil. An hour and fifteen minutes a day, five days a week, for nearly three months. She worked it out.

Seventy-five hours.

This diary contained the seventy-five hours spent with Thomas. How could she bring herself to put it next to her diaries from previous years?

She flicked through her new diary. Hours, days, months, but no Ts and no arrows.

A new year was about to begin.

She spent New Year with Bernard and Marie.

At midnight they exchanged kisses.

At that very moment, Thomas was kissing his wife, Claire was sure of it. A friend of Bernard's took her by the shoulders and kissed her on the mouth. She went along with it.

His name was Christophe. A little later, he insisted on taking her home. She agreed.

And she watched him opening the bottle of champagne she had bought for Thomas.

Before drinking, they clinked glasses.

He was bigger than Thomas, and much heavier.

*

Christophe was asleep.

Claire wasn't sleepy, so she got up silently and locked herself in the bathroom.

She was sorry she didn't smoke. If she had, she would have lit a cigarette and inhaled the smoke like that – she threw her head back and made a little 'o' with her mouth. She saw herself in the mirror and smiled. Should she change her hair-do? Shorter. Or longer. She blew out her cheeks and pulled some faces. Then she put on some make-up. Black on her eyes, red on her cheeks and on her lips. It was too much, it didn't suit her. And also, with all that red on her lips, how would she kiss Thomas? She took off her make-up and went back to bed.

The heat radiating from Christophe's body warmed her up again.

He went out to get some fresh bread for breakfast. From beside the bed Claire picked up three condom wrappers, empty, and threw them in the bin.

He put only one sugar in his coffee.

They went walking in the Bois de Vincennes and had lunch in a brasserie. Christophe ordered a *plateau de fruits de mer*. He shelled a crab and some prawns for Claire. She ate heartily and drank some white wine. Soon she would be having a siesta, alone. And tomorrow she would be seeing Thomas again.

She made her bed. On the bottom sheet she found some hairs belonging to Christophe.

He had seemed angry not to be going back up to her flat with her, and he had slammed the door of his car violently before setting off. Claire swept away the hair with the flat of her hand.

Why had she never managed to find so much as a single hair of Thomas's?

She went to bed, propping herself up on two pillows, and switched on the television, flicking from one channel to another.

Sometimes she slid her bare legs between the taut sheets. Sometimes she stretched.

Tomorrow she would be seeing Thomas again.

She woke up very early and immediately opened the window a little. She wanted to be sure of hearing the building-site work the minute it started again.

She washed her hair and got dressed. She would change quickly between two patients before Thomas arrived.

She frowned when she looked in the sink and saw the cup that Christophe had used at breakfast the previous day. She rinsed it and put it away. Then she toasted the rest of the bread he had bought.

After drinking her coffee and eating her toast, she ran the sponge over the table until all the crumbs had disappeared.

She changed the sheets. At lunchtime she would take them to the laundry.

Then there would be no trace of Christophe left.

She opened the window a little more, put a pullover around her shoulders because it was cold. And she waited for the noise from the building site.

She walked a patient to the door, and rushed back to listen to the messages on her personal answering machine.

At last she found one from Thomas. He would be coming at half-past seven. He hoped she would be there. He couldn't wait to see her again. The next patient rang the bell. She took out the cassette, slipped it into her pocket and replaced it with a new one. She ran to open the door.

Then she realized that she hadn't even listened to the other messages.

While the patient was undressing, she put the cassette in her desk drawer, careful not to put it on top of one of Thomas's dozen roses. She would have to put the flowers in a box to protect them.

She stroked the cover of her pharmaceutical dictionary. The few rose petals which had dropped off were hidden there; they were being pressed right in the middle, between 'lignocaine' and 'lymecycline'.

They didn't say a single word; they grasped each other with their hands. They were looking at each other, but they couldn't see; face against face, they were too close to see one another. They kissed.

First the gentleness of their teeth, the tender point of the canines and, further in, the hot surface of the molars. Then the sides, the smooth sides, where gum and enamel can sometimes be confused. And the inside of the cheeks, so soft that the palate seems hard and grainy in comparison. And the cool place, the narrow space between the upper lip and the gum, above the incisors.

They were rediscovering each other.

Thomas closed his arms around Claire. She suddenly realized that she was cold. How could she be cold when he was holding her so close to him? She slid her hands along Thomas's back. Beneath her fingers, beneath her palms, it was cold. It was leather, new. Thomas was wearing a new leather jacket. She pulled away from him and the leather gave a faint creak. She undid the zip of the jacket, freed Thomas's shoulders and pulled on the sleeves. The jacket didn't crumple. It fell on the floor, completely rigid.

They embraced again and she wasn't cold any more.

For the first time, Thomas stayed for an hour and a half.

He kissed her again on the landing.

Before the lift door closed again, Claire saw the jacket gleaming beneath the bright ceiling light.

She stayed motionless. The jacket must be a Christmas present, a present from his wife.

She felt a prickling under her bare feet and realized that she was standing on the doormat. She went back into her flat.

Claire imagined the two of them in the shop. Thomas was trying on jackets, one after the other. He wasn't saying anything, and his wife was giving her opinion. 'Turn round. No, too tight.' Finally she had said, 'That one.' The salesman assured them that the leather would get softer and shinier. Thomas kept the jacket on. He watched his wife with a smile. She was tapping in the code of her credit card. She was beautiful, the jacket would suit her too. He would lend it to her and the lining would be impregnated with her perfume.

Through the window, the salesman had watched them kissing. The woman's hands stroked the new leather.

Claire got dressed quickly. She had arranged to meet Marie in the restaurant.

In the metro, she sat on the fold-down seat near the door, on the platform side, facing forwards, her favourite seat.

She didn't yet know whether she would tell Marie about Thomas. And what would she say? 'We see each other for an hour and a quarter every day', and she would add, 'Except weekends.' She realized that she had never talked about him to anybody. She shook her head. Now that she was living with Bernard and had a child, Marie would certainly disapprove of a relationship with a married man from whom she could expect nothing. Claire decided not to tell her anything. She wondered if Thomas talked about her: 'I have a mistress.' She nearly burst out laughing. She repeated the words 'a mistress' several times, beneath her breath. A couple seated opposite her looked at her, so she stopped. But for the rest of the journey she couldn't help smiling.

*

The minute Marie arrived, Claire started talking about Thomas.

She told her how they had met. She told her that they embraced in the doorway, the door barely closed behind him, that they stayed glued to one another for more than an hour, and that she was happy. She broke off. Marie wasn't moving. She was staring at the bottle of wine. Claire poured herself a glass and put the bottle back at the other end of the table. But Marie didn't turn her head. She went on staring at the same point. She was probably trying to find a way of telling Claire to break it off. Claire drank her glass of wine. She raised her voice. Granted, she didn't know a lot about Thomas and she couldn't expect anything from him, but those moments were enough for her and she was happy. And that was that.

There was a silence. Marie raised her eyes. 'Great. And then maybe he'll leave his wife.'

Claire shrugged her shoulders. Nonsense – Thomas would never leave his wife, or his children.

It was impossible. She changed the subject. Why had she talked to Marie about Thomas?

Marie hardly ate anything and they parted early, though it was the first time they had had dinner since Marie had had her baby.

Before she went to bed, Claire had a bath.

At that time of the evening Thomas and his wife were probably coming back from dinner with friends. Thomas was driving, and his wife, tired, put her head on her husband's shoulder. She liked the cool contact of the new leather against her skin, she was drifting off to sleep. Very soon, when they got home, her skin would be imprinted with the seam of the jacket, and Thomas would press his lips to it.

So how could Marie say he might leave his wife? Had she been trying to encourage Claire to pursue the relationship? Claire tried to remember her intonation. 'Great. And then maybe he'll leave his wife.' Her tone was flat. It wasn't an encouragement. She remembered Marie's stare. And suddenly she remembered that Marie's hair had been dirty, and that she was very pale. Usually she wore make-up and, in all the fifteen years they had known each other, Claire had never seen her with dirty hair. And what about her lack of appetite? Why hadn't Claire noticed it all through dinner? It was obvious. Marie was suffering from post-natal depression after the birth of her baby.

She got out of her bath and quickly dried herself. She picked up the phone and then hung up immediately. She couldn't call Marie now – she would risk waking the baby. And Marie wouldn't talk if Bernard was there.

Claire sat down on her bed. She should have asked Marie some questions, got her to confide in her. If she was depressed, she must be having problems with Bernard. Claire froze. Marie had neither disapproved nor given her encouragement. She hadn't really been listening to her. And when she had said, 'Maybe he'll leave his wife,' she had been thinking about Bernard and herself. Not Thomas.

Claire went to bed.

Thomas wouldn't leave his wife.

She went to sleep.

Thomas wanted a drink.

Claire leapt out of bed and threw on her pullover.

Pulling open the sliding door to her little kitchen she wondered if he was watching her. She opened the fridge door. Her pullover was short, so she didn't bend over. She knelt down. She looked for the bottle of champagne and remembered she had drunk it with Christophe.

Fruit juice, beer, pastis, whisky?

She held her breath. At last she was going to find out what he liked.

Whisky.

He liked whisky. So did she.

She glanced at the clock on the coffee-maker.

Thomas had been there for an hour and ten minutes.

She pressed out some ice-cubes, refilled the ice tray and put it in the freezer. She took her time. Maybe he would stay for more than an hour and a half.

He had put his trousers on but his chest was bare.

He drank slowly. His Adam's apple rose and fell. He was talking about a site he had just started work on. Claire tried to listen to him, but couldn't. With every mouthful that Thomas swallowed she thought she could see the whisky flowing into his pharynx and then into his oesophagus. It passed behind the heart, through the diaphragm, and reached the stomach. And Claire's eyes followed it. Mouth, neck, chest, ribs, stomach.

Suddenly she wanted to kiss him again.

He left half an hour later.

What would he tell his wife? Throughout the journey, while he was driving, he would be thinking, trying to find excuses for being late. He would be driving fast on the icy road. And what if he had an accident? A serious accident, a fatal accident? Tomorrow and the day after, Claire would wait for him in vain. And then she would bump into one of the workmen in the street and he would tell her Thomas was dead. Unless work on the building site had stopped. She would go to the funeral. Only the labourers would recognize her, perhaps. From a distance she would see Thomas's wife and children and his family. Did he have brothers and sisters? She tried to imagine a sister for Thomas. Thomas as a woman, with long chestnut hair, a finer nose, a narrower mouth. She smiled. It didn't work. She would spot Thomas's in-laws, supporting their daughter. His mother-in-law was slim, she looked young. Thomas had always thought she was pretty. He told himself his wife would age as she had done. Claire's mother had never been beautiful, even in her youth.

Everyone would be given a rose. Could Claire ask for two? She would throw one on the coffin and keep the other one. It would be the last thing that she would put in her desk drawer. After that she would never add anything else.

October, November, December, the beginning of January. She would have known Thomas for barely three months, and those three months would be kept in a drawer.

Claire got dressed and went out.

It wasn't cold. So there would be no ice on the roads.

They had undressed and they were lying stretched out on the bed. Thomas pulled away from her. He didn't want to wear a condom any more, was that all right with her? Claire was about to say 'yes' when she thought about her desk drawer, the golden wrappers accumulating there, another one, sometimes two every day.

Without the condoms, what would she have left of the time she had spent with Thomas?

She refused.

He turned on his side and she heard the sound of paper tearing. Thomas would go on wearing condoms, and she would go on keeping the wrappers.

The next day she bought another bottle of champagne.

He didn't embrace her, he didn't kiss her.

He sat down on the bed and buried his face in his hands. Claire went over to him, touched his shoulder. What was happening?

She knelt opposite him, took his wrists to free his face. He went along with it, but turned his head away. He gently pushed Claire from him, and stood up. He remained motionless in the middle of the room. She watched him in silence, she didn't know what to say. She didn't understand.

Suddenly, he headed for the bathroom and

locked himself in. He stayed there for a long time. She heard him flushing the toilet. Then the tap ran in the basin.

When he reappeared, the curls that fell across his forehead were damp.

He took Claire by the arm, forced her to sit down. He had to talk to her. He had important things to say to her, very important things.

She waited. He seemed to be searching for the right words. His arms were pressed to him, as if he was cold.

She closed her eyes. She had understood. He was going to split up with her and was wondering how to tell her. He had a wife and kids; it was all too complicated. He had made up his mind he wasn't going to see Claire again. And yesterday, he hadn't wanted to wear a condom because it was the last time. She suddenly thought about the bottle of champagne cooling down in the freezer. It would explode. Good. Claire had bought it to drink with Thomas. She would never have drunk it without him.

Thomas's voice reached her, far away. She opened her eyes.

He turned his back on her. She began to stare at

the leather rectangle sewn on the waistband of his
jeans. She knew what Thomas was going to say, she
wasn't listening. She couldn't make out his size,
she screwed up her eyes. 'W33, L34.' The label
disappeared. Thomas had turned round again. And
then she heard what he was saying:

'I'm not married; I have no children.'

Claire thought she was smiling but Thomas
rushed towards her and she realized she was
crying.

She had buried her face in Thomas's neck. She
pressed herself to him, squeezed her thighs against
his, slid her feet between his. He was there, she
could hear him breathing. He was talking to her in
a low voice, telling her that now he was sure he
didn't want to leave her, ever.

An hour and a quarter, an hour and a half, more,
less, she would stop counting. He wasn't going to
leave.

The bottle of champagne hadn't blown up. Thomas
opened it.

Claire didn't throw away the cork.

Her hands were trembling. She looked at

Thomas. He wasn't married, he had no wife, no children. And as for the leather jacket, he had chosen it himself. She knocked over her champagne. Thomas took her glass from her.

'Let's go out.'

As soon as they were in the car Claire turned round and sniffed the head rest for the perfume of Thomas's wife.

She smiled. That was ridiculous – Thomas had no wife.

He turned on the ignition. She watched his wrist on the gear lever and the movement of his knees when he pressed one or other of the pedals.

She was beside him, in his car, a four-door with a telephone and, above it, the rectangular space for a car radio. They would listen to music together, and she would learn what he liked.

Her seat was too far back. She moved it forward and adjusted the seat-belt. Even yesterday she would have deduced that Thomas's wife was taller than she was, that her legs were longer.

But Thomas had no wife.

At a red light, Thomas drew her to him. Claire allowed herself to lean against the new leather jacket. And she pressed her cheek against the shoulder seam.

During dinner she didn't take her eyes off him.

He read the menu without moving it away from his face and without bringing it closer.

He chose herring with potato salad and steak *au poivre* with chips. He wasn't on a diet.

He ordered his meat rare.

He put some pepper on the herrings, salt on the chips. He took bread, lots of bread, and wiped his plate.

He ate quickly, exactly as she had imagined.

He had no dessert and put three sugars in his coffee.

She selected one from the sugar-bowl. On the paper wrapping there was a little clown.

She clutched it in her hand. It was their first dinner.

Although she was no longer hungry, she ordered a crème caramel so that she could stay a little longer, with Thomas, in the restaurant.

She was lying on her side. Thomas was sleeping pressed against her, his arm resting on Claire's arm, his hand clasping her wrist.

She smiled. The inside of her thighs was moist, a little sticky. Thomas hadn't used a condom; he never would again. She wanted to move her thighs and rub them together but she remained motionless. At her slightest movement Thomas might shift and pull away from her. And then she wouldn't feel his warmth against her back, or against her arm.

Claire fell asleep herself.

She saw Thomas and his long-haired wife. They were going to bed, he in his pyjamas, she in a big T-shirt because one of the two children would climb into their bed in the night.

She opened her eyes. Thomas had no wife and no children. He was sleeping next to her, pressed to her and his body was so warm that she was sweating. She began to breathe in the same rhythm as he did. She wasn't sleepy any more, she would not sleep.

She didn't want to miss any of that night.

They woke up very early.

Thomas's cheeks were rough. They felt good.

He drank a lot of coffee and ate several pieces of

toast that he dipped in his cup. Every time he poured some more coffee he took some sugar.

With him, a box of sugar would last only a fortnight.

At the supermarket, Claire would use a trolley.

He took her to visit the building site before the labourers got there.

It was still dark.

Thomas opened the little door in the hoarding and held Claire by the arm as they crossed the courtyard.

Inside the building, he switched on an inspection lamp. They climbed the stairs. Claire sniffed the air. It smelled of burning and dust, like Thomas's hair. She stopped and took a deep breath. She wanted to sit down there, on the steps, and stay there. She would close her eyes and over and over again she would breathe that smell, the smell of Thomas.

But he turned towards her and she had to go on climbing.

She got home just before her first patient arrived.

While she undressed, she put the champagne

cork and the previous day's sugar cube in her desk drawer.

The patient was coughing a lot. He had put his shirt on the chair in the surgery. Claire noticed that the collar and cuffs were dirty. She contemplated them for a moment. Soon, Thomas would be bringing clothes so that he could get changed. Shirts. Then she would get a washing-machine. He was sure to be able to install it himself, and then he would put a drying-rack up above the bath. That would be nice. She wouldn't wash anything by hand any more and she wouldn't go to the laundry. She would leave the doors open and the scent of the fabric conditioner would spread throughout the flat. And then their clothes would smell the same.

She put down her stethoscope. Bronchitis.

As soon as her patient had left she dashed to the bathroom. There was room for a washing-machine beside the basin.

Thomas lived in the suburbs, in a little house with a garden and a garage. He had bought it a year before and done it up himself.

They went in. Claire walked in slowly. Here was the drawing-room and the dining-room; over there, the kitchen. There were tiles on the floor, not carpet, and Thomas's voice echoed. Claire suddenly made for the kitchen. She tapped the wall. It wasn't a supporting wall. They could knock it down to make one big room.

Thomas came towards her. 'This summer we'll eat outside, in the garden.'

They kissed and went up to the first floor, to the bedroom.

*

Claire gently detached herself from Thomas and lay on her stomach.

She was going to sleep well.

He had said 'this summer' and 'we'. January, February, March, April, May, June. They wouldn't part for at least six months. 'We', she repeated to herself. From now on, Thomas and she would be 'we'. She closed her eyes. 'This summer we'll eat outside, in the garden.' Mild weather, a table and garden chairs in white plastic. Four chairs. Thomas's wife comes out of the kitchen.

Claire tried to find the switch for the bedside lamp. She must stop thinking about Thomas's wife. Thomas has no wife.

She got up. In the bathroom, she would probably find a sleeping pill.

The medicine cabinet contained a bottle of aspirin, some 90° alcohol and some sticking plaster. That was all. Claire smiled. Thomas never took any medicine. He was never ill.

She lay down next to him again, without turning out the light.

She watched him as he slept.

She decided to start seeing patients after seven again. She would work until half-past eight and then she would meet up with Thomas.

She would give him duplicates of her keys, so that he would be able to come in and wait for her last patient to leave.

No, she would rather he rang the bell, so that she could go and let him in and kiss him the minute the door had closed. As before.

She gave him the keys. It was simpler.

From now on she would double-lock the first drawer of her desk.

She was getting ready to have dinner at her flat with Thomas when she heard the phone ringing in her surgery. Although she wasn't on call, she hurried to answer it. It was bound to be an emergency. The answering machine started before she reached the phone, so she picked up the receiver and switched off the answering machine. It was one of her patients, Mme Corey. She was calling about her husband, who had a temperature and she was worried about him. She begged Claire to come at once – she didn't live far away. Claire jotted down the entry-code and the floor number and got her bag ready.

She told Thomas that she would be back soon.

He went with her to the door. He would wait until she got back before he had his dinner.

Mme Corey was waiting for her. Claire followed her down a long corridor and then into the bedroom. Claire liked the room immediately. She took off her coat and approached the big bed. In spite of the eiderdown and the heating, M. Corey was shivering. She reached out her hand to take his pulse, and even before she touched his wrist she could feel how hot his skin was.

His complexion was yellow. Claire pulled gently on his lower eyelid and pointed her torch at the white of the eye and the mucous membrane. They were yellow too. She noticed that he had long eyelashes.

She opened his pyjama jacket. The fabric was soft, flannelette.

He groaned when she palpated his liver.

She questioned him. Yes, he had felt nauseous for some days. Yes, his urine was very dark, he had noticed it that evening.

Claire took out her pad. Transaminase and bile pigment levels: she referred him for a number of different tests. No medication, just a little aspirin. It was probably viral hepatitis.

She put away her instruments and looked around at the walls covered with fabric, the carpet, the plump eiderdown. She turned to Mme Corey. 'I'll stay with him for a moment.'

The woman thanked her, murmured that she would wait in the drawing-room. And she left the room.

Claire settled down in an armchair beside the bed. She heard noises in the corridor. Little steps and children's voices. Two children. There was an irritated whisper. A door slammed.

Then nothing.

She put her hand on the sick man's forehead. His face contracted; his eyebrows and his hair tickled Claire's fingers to the rhythm of his spasms.

And then it was as if his forehead was expanding. The roots of his hair were no longer brushing Claire's little finger, and she no longer felt the caress of his eyebrows against her thumb. He had gone to sleep.

She only withdrew her hand when her arm started going to sleep.

He must be forty-five, a good ten years older than

his wife. Because of the perspiration that drenched his hair she couldn't tell what colour it was; it looked almost black.

He was tall. Why didn't she lie down next to him to see if he was much taller than she was? But she didn't move.

What was his first name? Before Corey, he would need a long Christian name, at least three syllables. Philippe, Jean-François, Dominique? She was beginning to get drowsy. She couldn't stay. But she was tired, she was sleeping so badly at night. And she liked this room so much. She closed her eyes.

A creak of the parquet floor woke her up. She got up just as Mme Corey was coming in. Claire set her mind at rest – everything would be fine.

She slipped her coat on and picked up her case, and they left the room.

As soon as she was in the lift, she unfolded the cheque that Mme Corey had given her. M. and Mme Jean-Philippe Corey. Three syllables. Claire had been right.

She ran back home. Her instruments rattled against each other in her bag.

*

With her fingers, Claire stroked Thomas's shoulder. His skin was smooth. Through flannelette it would seem even smoother.

She thought about M. Corey. With a fever like that, his body would heat up the bed so much in the night that his wife would probably throw the big eiderdown aside.

Claire went to sleep.

On Saturday, at the end of the afternoon, she went to Thomas's house. It was a short journey, twenty minutes by train. She brought some clothes that she would leave there. And some Valium, but she probably wouldn't need it. For the last two or three nights she had been sleeping better. She rested her head against the glass and then immediately sat up straight: she had forgotten to pay in the Corey's cheque.

Yes, it was still in her wallet, with the Polaroid of the drawer. She took out the photograph and gazed at it. She couldn't keep it – Thomas might find it one day. How would she explain to him that she kept all the wrappers of his condoms, and that she

105

had taken a photograph of them? And the sugar cubes? It was easy to make them out, little white rectangles.

She looked at the picture again, then she opened the bin fixed to the wall of the compartment. She threw in the Polaroid.

Soon she would replace it with a real photograph of Thomas. And she closed the lid.

The white dust fluttered about, like a fog. The furniture was covered with canvas sheets. There was rubble everywhere. Thomas had knocked down his kitchen wall.

There was rubble against her back and the canvas sheet was noisy but Thomas's lips tasted of plaster and Claire smiled against his mouth.

They went back to Claire's that evening. Thomas would stay there until his house was cleared up.

She got M. Corey's tests back. His wife had probably taken him to the laboratory.

A tourniquet above his elbow, an alcohol-drenched swab at the bend of his arm. 'Make a fist. That's right.' The needle approaches the vein, the skin soft, but yellow. His wife turns away; she probably can't bear the sight of blood.

It was hepatitis A, not too serious.

On the phone, Claire told Mme Corey that there wouldn't be any medication to take, no diet to follow. The patient could trust his own instinct, he wouldn't want to eat anything that might be harmful to him. He would need rest, a lot of rest. In three or

107

four weeks she would see him again and he would have more tests. She would authorize two months' sick leave from today.

Mme Corey interrupted her. Sick leave would be pointless. Her husband was a professional man, an architect.

Claire hung up.

M. Corey was an architect, like Thomas's wife.

But Thomas had no wife.

He always got up much earlier than she did, without using an alarm.

Sometimes she pretended to be asleep, and watched him.

He shaved, washed and dressed in less than a quarter of an hour, and ate his breakfast quickly.

Then he would approach the bed. Claire would try to stay motionless. He stayed there for a moment, leaning over her – she could feel his breath on her face – and then kiss her, lightly, on the cheek. A shift of air, he had stood up again. And then nothing, he was gone.

*

In the evening, he rarely came back before surgery hours were over.

From his office, his car or his house, he would call Claire to tell her when he would be back, and although he had the keys he rang the doorbell, so that the minute she opened the door to him they embraced.

There was no more rubble, no more sheets and no more dust.

Thomas had converted his kitchen and, where the wall had been, he had built a wide counter on which they were having their dinner for the first time this evening.

Lying on the sofa, Claire watched him preparing the meal, a Hungarian dish with sauerkraut. He poured in some white wine. It smelled good. She laid her head back on the cushion. M. Corey wouldn't be able to bear that smell, it would make him nauseous. At that moment, his wife was probably peeling vegetables to make him a soup. And in a minute, at the table, he would blow on each spoonful before bringing it to his mouth. The children were having fun imitating him. 'That's enough now, don't forget that daddy's poorly.'

Then Claire wondered if Nicolas would like Thomas.

Of course he would.

M. Corey phoned her to make an appointment.

'Tomorrow at four?'

'Perfect. Thank you, Doctor.'

'Doctor.' She remembered the day when Thomas had addressed her like that. It was in the street. 'Doctor.' And he had run to meet her.

M. Corey had said 'Doctor' as if he was speaking to an older person. When she had gone to examine him, he had been so feverish that he probably hadn't seen her. If he had seen her he wouldn't remember it.

But on the phone, by the tone and timbre of her voice, he must have realized that she was a young woman.

She said a few sentences out loud, the first things that came into her head.

Her voice was a young woman's voice.

If he had called her himself, maybe he would come alone, without his wife.

In her appointments book, on the page for the following day, at four, Claire wrote: 'J.-P.C.'

They woke up at the same time and had breakfast together.

When Thomas held her in his arms, Claire's dressing-gown fell half open. The leather of his jacket was supple and warm against her skin.

She washed her hair, dried it and slipped on her short skirt and her black jumper. She picked up her bottle of eau de toilette. It was almost full. Thomas hated perfume. She brought it to her neck and changed her mind. With hepatitis you never knew. The scent, however delicate, might bother M. Corey.

*

Claire accompanied her patient to the door, and then put on her make-up.

Ten to four. It took five minutes to get from the Coreys' on foot. M. Corey would still be very tired, and it would, in all probability, take him ten minutes.

Now, he's putting on his fur-lined jacket, knotting his scarf and leaving his flat. He gets into the lift. His wife stops him, she hands him his gloves. He thanks her and kisses her. What would he do without her?

The cold air does him good. He crosses the street, turns left, goes straight on. Passing by the *traiteur*'s shop window, he pulls a face. The sight of the Piedmontese salad makes him feel ill. And the swirls of mayonnaise on the crayfish? He turns his eyes away. He stops at the kiosk and buys his evening paper, so as to have something to read if the doctor keeps him waiting.

Claire headed for the door; she wouldn't keep him waiting, she would see him straight away.

Five to four. He's probably reached the building-site hoarding. Maybe he was the architect of the building. No, Thomas had spoken of an Italian architect.

Still fifty yards to go. He hoists up his trousers as he walks. Since the beginning of his illness, he must have lost over half a stone. He will try not to put it on again.

Under the porch he hesitates. Which floor? He looks for the brass plaque. Third floor. He calls the lift.

Claire listened to the noises of the staircase. She couldn't hear anything.

M. Corey rang ten minutes later.

He wasn't wearing a fur-lined jacket, but a coat.

A newspaper stuck out of his pocket.

He was very tall, and very dark. His red and black checked shirt looked as if it was flannelette.

He smiled at her while she examined him. He couldn't remember her but he remembered the coolness of her hand on his forehead as he had gone to sleep.

Claire pulled up M. Corey's eyelid, and she thought his eye was staring at her. She pointed her torch at it.

Not a trace of yellow.

He got dressed again and she prescribed a series of tests.

Could he go back to work?

She would rather he rest for at least another fortnight. He had to be sensible, she insisted. And of course, not a drop of alcohol.

'Very good, Doctor.' This time, he had said 'Doctor' with a smile.

He took his cheque-book from his pocket and Claire heard something fall on the floor.

He didn't notice, and she didn't say anything.

On the landing he shook her hand.

Claire quickly went back into her surgery. What had he dropped? She bent down and found a book of matches. On the flap there was the name of a restaurant.

She sat down, leant her chin on her palms and stayed like that, motionless.

Finally she got up; her next patient would be there soon.

She opened the top drawer of her desk and plunged her hand inside.

The pieces of gold paper rustled under her fingers.

She took the drawer out of the desk and put it on her knees. The little clown on the sugar cube from their first dinner smiled at her.

Now she had dinner with Thomas every evening and soon they would live together. She would become his wife. And they would have children.

She grabbed the drawer and tipped it over the waste-paper basket. She tipped it a little more, and then some more again, and the gold wrappers, the sugar cubes, the dozen dried roses, the champagne cork, the Polaroids, the answering-machine cassettes and the little yellow plastic golf club slipped gently into the bin-liner.

Claire slid the empty drawer back in place and put M. Corey's book of matches inside. Then she locked it.

And she smiled.